PARKER FEELINGS

by **Parker Curry & Jessica Curry**
illustrated by **Brittany Jackson & Tajaé Keith**

Ready-to-Read

Simon Spotlight

New York London Toronto Sydney New Delhi

For my mom
—P. C.

For my godmother, CynD,
who helped me manage my big feelings as a little girl
—J. C.

SIMON SPOTLIGHT
An imprint of Simon & Schuster Children's Publishing Division
1230 Avenue of the Americas, New York, New York 10020
This Simon Spotlight edition December 2023
Manufactured in the United States of America 1123 LAK • 10 9 8 7 6 5 4 3 2 1
Library of Congress Cataloging-in-Publication Data
Names: Curry, Parker, author. | Curry, Jessica, author. | Jackson, Bea, 1986– illustrator. | Keith, Tajaé, illustrator.
Title: Parker's big feelings / by Parker Curry & Jessica Curry; illustrated by Brittany Jackson & Tajaé Keith.
Description: New York : Spotlight, 2023. | Series: Ready-to-read: Level 1 | Audience: Ages 4 to 6. |
Summary: With a little help from her mom, Parker tries to turn a bad day into a good one.
Identifiers: LCCN 2023009026 (print) | LCCN 2023009027 (ebook)
ISBN 9781665942768 (hardcover) | ISBN 9781665942751 (paperback) | ISBN 9781665942775 (ebook)
Subjects: CYAC: Emotions—Fiction. | Life skills—Fiction. | LCGFT: Picture books.
Classification: LCC PZ7.1.C8665 Pb 2023 (print) | LCC PZ7.1.C8665 (ebook) | DDC [E]—dc23
LC record available at https://lccn.loc.gov/2023009026
LC ebook record available at https://lccn.loc.gov/2023009027

My name is Parker.
I am the new kid in school.

Today our teacher says,
"Pick a partner."

No one picks me.
I miss my bestie,
Gia!

At lunch I spill juice on my new shirt.

At recess I fall
on the playground.
I wish this day was over!

When I get home I grab the book Gia and I are reading. Then I find a quiet spot.

But Ava and Cash want to play, and they chase me into my room.

"Leave me alone!" I say.

"Is everything okay, Parker?"
Mom asks.

"I miss Gia! I miss Papi!
I miss my old school!" I cry.

"Those are big feelings,"
says Mom.

We write a list of things
I can do to feel better.

I close my eyes.
I breathe in.
I pretend I am smelling a
flower as I count to five.

1.Breathe

Now I breathe out.
I pretend I am blowing
out a candle.

Wow! I am feeling better!

2.Exercise

"Exercising helps turn on
happy feelings,"
says Mom.
I put on my bike helmet.

I ride up and
down the block!
Whee!

"Parker needs time alone," Mom tells Ava and Cash.

We set up a reading nook with an owl timer!

I set my timer
before I start reading.

When the timer hoots
I ask Ava and Cash,
"Want to play?"
"Yes!" they shout.

"Are you feeling better?" asks Mom.

You bet!

BIG HELP FOR BIG FEELINGS!

In this book, Parker's day is not going very well. She deals with lots of big feelings. Have you ever experienced big feelings like sadness, anger, jealousy, frustration, disappointment, or fear? Everyone feels those emotions at some point or another.

Sometimes it can seem like those feelings are here to stay. But big feelings don't last forever. There are even some things you can do to help yourself feel better.

Parker's mom helped her feel better in this story by reminding her to breathe, exercise, and take some time for herself. When Parker did those things, she felt a lot better.

There are other things you can do too, like thinking of what makes you happy or taking some time to count to yourself, color, or listen to music. You might also want to talk to a trusted friend or adult about why you are feeling this way and what would help you feel better.

The next time you feel big emotions, try some of these things. Then think about how you feel afterward. Hopefully you'll feel better soon!